EIGHTEEN YEARS

AMANDA FISHER

PublishAmerica
Baltimore

Softcover 9781630047306
PUBLISHED BY PUBLISHAMERICA, LLLP
www.publishamerica.com
Baltimore

Printed in the United States of America

CHAPTER 1

October 12, 1989—7:47 pm

I open my eyes and see a face. It's her face. My mom. We are in a bright room with bright lights and light colored walls. I hear beeps and when mom lifts her hand to stroke my cheek, she has an IV tube in her arm. and a bracelet on her wrist. She speaks to me with a beautiful voice. I could hear her voice muffled when I was in her womb, but this is my first time hearing her for real. I tried to smile to show my excitement, but my body does not respond the way I was hoping. I could feel other people come into the room, but never took my eyes off mom. The others came around the bed. One was young like me, but bigger and could control her body. The other one had a wrinkly face, a big shoulder bag, and smelt, not normal.

The young one had gotten closer and was moving in such a way as if taking me from mom. I was on the verge of crying, but then she spoke in the same tone as mom. She slowly rocked me in her arms, and then sat down. I was so comfortable I slowly went to sleep.

When I woke, I saw a different face. It was the wrinkly one that smelt not normal. Her voice was soft, but a little shakier than mom.

Mom and I spent a few more days in the hospital. The young girl came back when mom was putting stuff in bags. Mom carried the bags and of course the girl carried me. We went into the box in the wall that brought us to a different floor. When we stepped out of the box, everything seemed brighter. My eyes were really sensitive to the light. The girl looked down at me and covered my eyes. The next thing I knew was a different smell. It was a cleaner, fresher smell. The girl took her hand away from my eyes and put me in a comfy thing with straps. The door made a loud noise when she pulled it shut. The old one turned her hand and the box on wheels turned on. The young girl rolled down her window and I felt the air.

I had gone to sleep and woke up to the girl picking me up. She looked down at me, and her lips moved, but I didn't understand. Mom went through the door first, then me and the girl, then the old person. This was a whole new place to look at. I heard a deep noise come from another room. It was a very different sound then what the girl made. We went to the room and another big person was there, but it didn't look like mom, or the girl. It got up and came closer. It looked down at me with mean eyes. It looked to mom and made that deep noise again. It left the room, leaving a not so fresh smell behind. The girl took me back outside and looked down at me.

7 months
I was in my very own little box in the house. It was bright with color. The blankets and lifeless animals were soft and mom was warm when she held me. She was dressing me and putting heavy shoes on my feet. They made a sound when I tried to get away from mom. I loved running from her. She would chase after me, pick me up and blow on my tummy. It tickled. When I laughed, she laughed, and then the deep voice person would yell. I haven't seen the girl for a while. I miss her. Her voice was much more gentle than the deep voice person.

11 months

Mom was sitting in the rocking chair in my room and I was on her lap. We were looking at a book with people in rectangles, that weren't moving. "Mama," I said pointing to a picture. She would talk to me then I would point to another picture.

"Dada," I said pointing to a picture.

"Dada," she repeated. She smiled and kissed me gently on the head. I looked to her.

"Dada," I said pointing to the door. She moved her head up and down and looked back to the book with no smile. I pointed to another picture.

"Your sister," mom said.

"Sis-sis," I tried.

She smiled again. "Shellie."

I turned to the book not going to even try saying it. The end of the book came and she closed it and turned it over to see the cover again. I lay on her chest and she held me closer. She ran her fingers softly through my hair.

I could see that my light was still on through my closed eyes. I sat up and I was in my crib. I could hear mama talking in a hushed, hurt tone. I heard dada's voice.

"Mama," I said.

The house became quiet. I heard slow, quiet footsteps. Mama came to the door. Her eyes were red and puffy, and her face looked wet. She came over and picked me up. I touched her cheek. "Mama."

She hugged me tight and I laid my head on her shoulder. She sat down in the rocking chair and was talking to me again. Her soft, gentle voice put me to sleep.

1 year

I woke up every night, half way through the night. I could always hear mom talking quietly, as if trying not to wake me. She would come in hoping I was still asleep, but I never was.

A year had passed since the first time I saw my mom. Her and I had our own little party because today was my birthday and mama made it a special day for me. I blew out a candle and ate sweet tasting food with her. By the time night fell I was starting to see that the mom I met a year ago was different. She is not as strong as she was before. It was like something has beaten her down.

CHAPTER 2

I was playing with blocks in my room when I heard Sissy's voice. She was talking to mama. I tried running, but my little, stubby legs made me wobble instead. I stood in the doorway to Sissy's room. They were sitting on her bed. Sissy looked over at me. She slowly stood up and as she got closer I could see her eyes were wet. She picked me up and hugged me tight.

"I'm sorry," she said. "So sorry."

"Sissy?"

She looked at me and we sat on the bed. I jumped to the sound of dada's voice and pushed myself closer to Sissy. She looked down at me. "It's okay."

She held me tighter, and then dada appeared in the doorway. He didn't look very happy. He came in and grabbed mom by the wrist.

"Stay here," she said as dad was pulling her out of the room. She closed the door behind her. Sissy ran over and locked the door. She came back over to me and hugged me like she never has before. I could hear dada yelling again.

"It's not my fault," mama said.

I looked up at Sissy. Her emotion went from being scared to being protective. She picked me up and put me on the bed. "Stay here."

She opened the door and ran to where she heard mom. I got off the bed and walked to where I could see what was happening. I knew dada could yell, but this was a whole new side to him I was seeing. I walked to behind the couch then peeked up over the arm of it. I saw Sissy by the fireplace not moving. I went over to her. I felt someone pick me up.

"Noo," mom screamed.

Then I realized dada was holding me. He walked quickly into his room and locked the door behind him. He dropped me on the bed and I heard something slam into the door.

"No, please. You can have anything but her," mom pleaded.

"Anything," dada questioned.

Sissy slowly came in and ran over to me. Dada held her back and tied her in a chair. Then he wrapped a band around her arm. He held something pointy in one hand and Sissy looked at me as a tear ran down her cheek.

Mom finally burst through the door. "You've done it to me before. Why don't you do it again?"

"Mama," I cried.

"It's okay baby."

Mom stayed between dada and Sissy. I looked around mama and Sissy was trying to stay awake. Mom turned around and untied Sissy and brought her into her room. I followed close behind.

Mama picked me up and put me on the bed next to Sissy. I put my hand on her shoulder and looked to mom.

"She's okay baby. Come here," she said.

I crawled over to mama's lap and she held me. She started telling me a story about her and dada. They didn't want to have Sissy and now that I was here he was as mad as ever. Mama can only protect us for so long. I heard Sissy say something. I moved to her head and lay next to her. Mom lay on the other side of me after closing and locking the door.

I had taken a short nap, but Sissy was still asleep when I woke up. Mom was sitting by the window. We heard a door slam shut, and finally everything was quiet. Mom went over to the door and opened it. I stayed by Sissy and she eventually woke up.

"Hey," she said.

"Hi Sissy," I said happy.

"Where you go?" I asked.

"Away with friends."

"You gone to long. I miss you."

"I know. I will never leave you again. You and mom, I will never leave again." She hugged me and picked me up. "Let's go to the playground."

"What that?"

"Come on. I will show you," she said.

We went to the playground, and a few other places. Mama and Sissy are always taking me places. I had a great second birthday. Sissy got me the best gift ever. She got me a new teddy bear. I felt the happiest person on earth.

CHAPTER 3

"What is this?"

"Dad I—I don't know. I don't know what happened. I'll bring it up."

"You said that last time."

"That was a different class," Sissy begged.

I was standing at the end of the hallway looking into the living room. Mom looked over at me. She ran over and scooped me up. She put me in my crib, locked and closed the door.

"She will bring the grade up," mom said. "She's done it before."

"She said last time it wouldn't happen again."

"Well if her home life was better, maybe she could focus more on school."

I heard my door handle twist and sissy came in. "Hey, you okay?"

"Yes, I'm scared. Are you?"

"I can't be scared. I need to be brave for you and mom," she said.

"Are you scared?" I asked again.

"Yes Mattie. It will be okay though. Mom says that if he hurts either one of us he will be going to jail for child abuse."

"What about mama?"

"We can help her as much as we can. She's doing it to protect us."

Sissy sat in the rocking chair and put me on her lap. She covered my ears, but I could still hear dada.

"Are you saying this is my fault?"

"Yes, that's exactly what I am saying," mom said raising her voice. "If you weren't all hyped up on drugs and alcohol, you would know what goes on in her life, but you don't. All you seem to do around here is hurt me and scare them. I have had enough."

Sissy tightened her hug around me. "I will never leave you. I will never let go. Not again. I'm sorry."

"Sissy, Sissy."

"Mommy, she yelled. "Mom, mom."

She placed me on the floor, and lay down next to me. "Go get mom. Mommy."

I wobbled to the door and reached for the knob, but couldn't reach it. I got the stool that was next to my dresser and cracked the door open. I ran through the house. "Mommy, mommy."

"In here Mattie."

I ran to her room. She was strapped to the bed. Her wrists were tied to the posts. "Pull on the rope for me sweetie. Where is your sister?"

"My room," I said.

Mommy picked me up. Sissy was in worse shape than before. Mommy knelt down beside her. "Shellie, baby. It's okay. Daddy is gone. We are safe. You did good. You protected your sister. Come back to me baby. Your sister needs you."

Mom picked Sissy's head up and stroked her cheek and ran fingers through Sissy's hair. I knelt down and held Sissy's hand. Mom grabbed a paper bag from my bottom dresser drawer.

"Breath into this hunny. Relax baby. We are right here."

A short while after, Sissy was asleep on mom's lap. Mom kept looking down at her, stroking her hair. She looked up at me and patted the floor next to her. I put my hand on top of mom's hand and went to sleep.

I woke in a dark room. An arm was over me. Whoever was next to me started having a bad dream. It was Sissy.

"Mommy. Don't hurt me. Daddy don't, mommy help me."

"Sissy, it's a dream. Wake up."

She yelled and sat up. The bedroom door flung open. The light turned on and mom came to the rescue again. "Shhh, shh, shh, it's okay Shellie. Mom is here."

"Mommy," she said, her eyes slowly looking up to meet mom's eyes. Then Sissy looked down at me. "I didn't mean to wake anyone else."

"Shh, hunny,"

"Mommy," she said drifting back off.

"You go back to sleep too," she looked to me. I lay on Sissy's shoulder and looked at mom until I went to sleep.

Sissy's bad dreams had gotten worse. During the day when dad wasn't home she was a different person. She was strong and protective. At night she seemed so, helpless, always looking for mom's gentle touch.

My third birthday did not consist of gifts this year. It was of cupcakes and a day out with mom and Sissy.

On my birthday we got home after a fun day and dad had hurt mom like always. I think I shocked him when I had enough. I stood in between him and mom, and he stopped immediately. He had left that day and hasn't come back since. Mom put the house up for sale and we've been packing.

CHAPTER 4

The old lady who I saw when I first lay eyes on this world opened the door.

"Hi grandma," Sissy said. There was no kiss and no hug. Grandma just moved aside and Sissy went in. Mom pushed me ahead of her and made slight eye contact with grandma as she walked by.

"Why are you here?" grandma asked.

"We sold the house."

"Why?"

"Because I don't ever want to remember anything that went on in that house."

"Oh, well okay. The three of you will have to share a room. I haven't gotten the chance to clean out the spare room."

"That's fine. The girls can share I'll sleep on the couch if that's okay."

"Fine, so, where's Roger?"

"He left. He was drunk again. Don't know where he is." Mom looked at Sissy and me. "You two should get to sleep. You will be safe here. Off to bed."

"I want you to come mommy," I said.

"I'll be in a little later. You and Sissy go."

Sissy picked me up and we went to the room set up for us. We changed into pajamas and Sissy fell onto the bed in exhaustion. She looked at me through her half open eyes and patted the spot next to her. I cuddled up next to her. I was facing her body, with her arm under my head and an arm over me, keeping me safe. I started playing with her hair because I couldn't sleep. Sissy on the other hand was already out cold. I looked up to her face. She seemed to finally be at peace.

I had just closed my eyes and heard footsteps beyond the doorway. I sat up and mom was still not here. I wobbled to the door and the TV was still on. I slowly walked out and mommy was asleep on the couch. I climbed up next to her.

"Mommy." I got no response. I moved her arms so they wrapped around me. "Mommy."

"Mattie." I looked up to her. "Why aren't you with your sister?"

"I got scared."

"Scared of what baby?"

"My bad dreams. Sissy's bad dreams."

"We are safe here. You need to go to sleep. Here, come sleep on my chest. You've always gone to sleep with a heart beat."

Mom's hands were now on my lower back. I found a piece of her hair to play with. I heard the TV go off and opened my eyes. The room was dark and quiet except for mom's breathing. I tried to block out the quiet by listening to mom's heartbeat. I closed my eyes and it felt like I was back inside mommy's tummy.

I woke up and through the window I could see light on the horizon. I turned my head to face the back of the couch. Mommy turned to her side and placed me next to her. I was quite comfortable pinned between mom and the couch. I saw the necklace on her neck and gently took hold of it. It was very pretty. I snuggled up against mom and tried for another round of sleep.

"Mattie," someone yelled. The yell woke me out of sleep. I looked up to mom. She was awake now. She slowly got up and went to see Sissy. I followed her. I stood at the doorway while mommy went in to calm her down.

"Mommy."

"Shellie, Mattie is safe." Mom waved me over. "Open your eyes Shellie. Mattie is right here."

"Sissy, I'm right here." I touched her hand, but she pulled away. I looked to mommy and was on the edge of crying.

"Give her time," mom said.

I sat back and let mom take care of Sissy. I got up after a while and went back out to the couch. I heard plates hit each other from the kitchen area.

I went to the kitchen and slowly walked in. "Hey there little one."

"Grandma," I said lifting my arms. She picked me up and sat me on her lap as she sat in the chair.

"Where's mom?" she asked. I pointed to the door. "I'll be right back."

I felt to small to be sitting at a big person table. I looked out the window and stood up to get the whole view. We were high up. Mom and grandma came back in.

"Sissy?"

"She went back to sleep darling. You can see her after breakfast."

Grandma made really good pancakes I went to see Sissy. I quietly wobble over to her and sat down. She had ended up on the floor. I touched her hand and kissed her cheek. She slowly opened her eyes. "Hey."

"Hey Sissy. You okay?"

"Yeah, had another, oh never mind." She sat up and I pulled her to the kitchen.

"Pancakes," I said.

Sissy and I were on the balcony. She was bouncing me on her knee. It was fun, but I had to keep my mouth closed to keep from biting my tongue. I've done that more then once and it hurt. In the middle of one of my bounce times, I could hear mommy and grandma arguing in the kitchen.

"Well, you wouldn't be staying here if you had money."

"I would have money if I could stop having kids and get a job. You know, you just think that life with Roger is so easy. It wasn't, it isn't. He's abusive to me, he scared my daughters and now he has pretty much taken our home. Now, I don't know about you, but I refuse to let my girls grow up on the street."

"So get a job."

"Fine I will."

The house echoed as a door was slammed shut. Sissy stood up and put me on her hip and went to the door to the kitchen. "Where mama going?"

"I don't know," Sissy said. "Let's go for a walk. You can ride in the stroller."

We were walking and Sissy was talking to me like she always did when she felt overwhelmed. I lay my head back in the stroller and let sleep take me. I started having a bad dream, and daddy was in it.

I slowly opened my eyes and Sissy was holding me. "I had a bad dream."

"I know. You're okay. You were talking in your sleep. Everything is okay. You know that right?"

I lay my head against her shoulder. "I miss mommy."

"Maybe she's back at grandma's. You want to go see?" She put me back in the stroller and put the hood of the stroller up. I looked up and could see Sissy through the hood of the stroller.

Mommy was on the couch when we got back. I wobbled over to her. "Mommy."

She picked me up. "Mommy where did you go?"
"I went for a walk."
"Don't lie to her," grandma said.
"She won't know the difference."
"She won't, but I will," Sissy said. "I heard you guys fighting. Why don't you have a job?"
Mom never answered the question.

My birthday wasn't like my normal birthdays. I didn't get anything wrapped in pretty paper, or covered in ribbons, but grandma made her special pancakes for me for breakfast. Mom wasn't home on my birthday, but Sissy was and that made me happy enough.

CHAPTER 5

Mommy was holding me against her chest. "Do you want to know why I don't have a job? It's because after I had Shellie, Roger was upset because he wanted a son. It was no more then two weeks after we brought Shellie home we were trying for another baby. We tried for seven years and all of the ones that had started to grow had been miscarriages. Of the few that made it to the point where I could tell the gender, I had two boys, and they didn't make it pass the third month. That man kept trying until this little miracle happened." She looked to me and I wiped a tear from her cheek. She hugged me tight. "But Roger didn't exactly welcome her into the family."

"Roger is gone, so it's time to start a new. Start it off right. Get a job so your daughters can have a memorable childhood," grandma said.

"One problem," mom said. "I didn't go to college, so the best I could get is a cashier."

"You know the liquor store is looking for someone."

"Yeah, you don't remember my drinking problem in high school."

"That was eighteen years ago. Have you had a drink since?"

"Well, I officially gave it up three years before I had Shellie."

"So, what's the problem?"

"I don't want the urge to come back."

"It's not about you anymore. Do what's best for your girls," grandma said sternly. She left the room and Shellie came over and sat next to mom. Mom laid my head against her chest. Shellie held mom's hand.

"What else have you been hiding from me?" Shellie asked.

"Nothing."

"Mom, I know I'm not even a teenager yet, but I think I have had to grow up faster than a normal twelve year old."

"Honestly Shellie. I'm not hiding anything else."

Shellie kissed mom's forehead and went into her room. Mom lay back on the pillows and stroked my hair. I was trying so hard to fight sleep, but I felt mom relax and sleep snuck up on me.

I woke up from another bad dream. The room was dark. I sat up and Sissy's light was still on. I gently got off mom and went to Sissy's room. I stood in the doorway. The light was on, but Sissy was asleep. I went over to her bedside. The undersides of her eyes were red, so I knew she had been crying I climbed up onto the bed next to her and wrapped her arms around me. She squeezed me tight.

"Sissy, the light is still on." I didn't get a response back. "Okay, we will leave it on."

I turned over to face her and suddenly felt safe. Sleep came fast and so did the dream.

I woke to Sissy saying my name. I slowly opened my eyes. "Sissy."

"I'm right here Mattie."

"I saw daddy again. He hurt us."

"Mattie," she said turning my head to face her. "That will never happen again. Daddy is gone. We are safe. You are safe."

The tears were running like a waterfall now. "I want mommy."

Sissy carried me out to mommy. I could hear mommy's soft breathing. Sissy gently laid me on mommy's chest and I was out like a light.

I was the first one up the next morning. Sissy was on the floor next to us. I lay back down on mommy and looked down at Sissy. Her eyes were still red. I want to help her, but she likes to be alone when she has her breakdowns.

"Sissy," I said walking into her room. She was wiping away tears. "Sissy?"
"I'm okay."
"Why you crying?"
"I wasn't. I'm not."
"Let me help."
She tapped the bed next to me. We leaned against the wall and all her feelings came out.

Mom and grandma had left for something. Shellie had worked herself into a panic attack and I didn't know what to do. At least she was letting it out. She has had these emotions locked up for nearly five years, but the emotions are all coming out at the same time.

Mom had come back in the middle of the Sissy's attack. Sissy had yelled for mom as soon as she heard the door open. Mom quickly came in. My legs were stuck under Sissy's shoulders. I had started crying because I was scared for Sissy. Mom came over to us and lifted Sissy's body up. I got my legs back and lay next to Sissy. "Mommy, I don't want her to hurt anymore."

"I know Mattie. This is my fault. I couldn't protect you guys from his verbal violence." Mommy looked down at Sissy and grandma came to the door.

"That's not true," Grandma said. "I'm sorry about what I said before. You can stay as long as you need, just as long as you have a job. The liquor store wants you. Make it worth their wild to keep you." She smiled then left.

Sissy was asleep and I was close to sleep as well. Mom touched my cheek and I looked up to her with tired eyes. "Go to sleep baby. You definitely need it after last night." She didn't have to tell me twice. My eyes slowly closed. I could feel my hand on Sissy's tummy move with the pattern of her breathing. I put my head on her shoulder hoping to hear the beating of her heart. I did and that put me right to sleep.

CHAPTER 6

Mom was at work and grandma, Sissy and me were having dinner. I turned five last month, but it wasn't exactly one I want to remember.

I was looking down at my plate and started crying for no reason. The tears started slowly then dripped onto my plate.

"Mattie." I looked up at Sissy.

"This is what dad has done to us."

She got up and put me on her lap. She held me to her chest and I could hear her heartbeat. I calmed down and climbed off her and went into Sissy's room. I lay on her bed and could hear grandma and Shellie quietly starting to argue. I put the pillow over my head and waited.

"So did you mean it when you apologized to mom before," Sissy said louder.

"I only apologized because it felt like the right thing to do. No I do not believe that your father is abusive in the way she is saying."

"Why not?"

"The day they got married your mother was the happiest person on earth. Roger was the ultimate match for her. They were perfect for each other. There was no other man like him."

"Marriage can change people though. The pressure of a household and a family was clearly to much for him."

"Get out," grandma yelled.

"It's not my fault you won't believe your own daughter. You have been blind to her ever since I was right."

"Get out of my sight." I heard skin in skin contact and closed my eyes tight.

"Mattie," I uncovered my head and Shellie was holding her cheek. She came over and sat on the bed. I took her hand away. There were five fingers imprinted on her skin. I heard the door open. Shellie got up and went to the doorway. She ran out into the living room. Mom was home. I went to the doorway of our room and saw mommy looking at Sissy's cheek.

"What happened?"

"Grandma and I got into an argument."

"She hit you?"

"Well Mattie can't hit this hard, nor would she."

"Go in with your sister," she told Sissy.

I went back to Sissy's bed and waited for her to come in. She held me as we leaned against the wall. I lay on her lap and looked up at her. She had wet and dry tears on her cheeks. The tears on the right side of her face were starting to moisten the forming bruise on her cheek.

"Do you think mommy protected us because grandma abused her when she was little?" I asked.

"Maybe," Sissy said lying down.

She laid me down with her and I heard mommy talking to grandma.

"Don't you ever lay a hand on her again."

"Or what? You didn't fight back when you were little. Will you fight back now?"

"No, you're my mother and I respect you."

The house got quiet. Sissy's breathing broke the silence. She was dreaming. Mom passed by the doorway, but didn't look in. I turned over to feel safe against Sissy's body. I felt so warm and safe, but sleep never came.

CHAPTER 7

My sixth birthday seemed like just an ordinary day in the year. Even Sissy forgot it. Mom has been very different lately. She still has the liquor store job, but she's not herself at all. It's like her emotions have gone down the drain. It's been a year in a half since I've seen a smile let alone a laugh. Her and grandma stayed distant from each other ever since the incident with Shellie.

I was lying with Sissy. We were both staring at the ceiling in silence. I looked over at her and saw tears working their way down to her hairline. "I can't."

"Talk to me," I said.

"I need to get out. I have to find a way to live on my own. Mom is going into a depression Mattie, and she is not going to come out of it.

"But she loves us?"

"Yeah, she loves us, but it's not the mom we know."

I went out to mom and she was sitting on the couch. I saw grandma at the kitchen table when I walked by. I stood in front of mom, and grandma stood in the doorway of the kitchen looking out at me. I saw Sissy appear in the doorway or her room. I looked to mom and it felt like she was looking through me, not at me.

"Mom." I got nothing. I touched her hand. "Mom, look at me." I pulled her face down to me. I heard grandma come over.

"Mattie, mom is tired. Go back in with Shellie."

"No, I want mommy." I looked back to mom.

"I want my Mattie," mom said.

I went over to her and climbed up next to her. She lay down and I put her arms around me. Grandma left the room and I found mom's necklace. I held onto it like there was no tomorrow.

I woke up and mommy was having a nightmare. I quickly got off the couch and yelled for grandma. The lights went on and Sissy came out too.

"It's not a nightmare. It's a seizure."

Grandma went to her head and put pillows around it. Sissy held me on the opposite wall. "It's my fault."

"Grandma?"

"Shellie, hunny. I am so sorry I hit you the way I did."

"Did you abuse mom?"

There was a silence in the room.

"Mattie."

"Mommy," I said running to her side.

"You need to leave with your sister. Mommy is gone," she said. My knees collapsed beneath me and I fell to all fours.

"No." I looked up to grandma. "No, you need to get through this. You need to be there for your daughters. You can't give up on the hardest job in the world. You signed up the day you had Shellie, and you cannot sign off until you have taught your girls everything they need to know."

Shellie picked me up and put me in the chair. Tears were streaming down my cheeks as I looked at mom. Mom looked up at grandma, and then turned away. Grandma took us into our room.

"Did you abuse mom?" Shellie asked again.

"Yes," she confessed. "I never wanted to hurt her. My father abused me physically, mentally and emotionally. I had made a commitment to myself that I would never lay a hand on my child. There was one year something in me just snapped and

I hit her. I loved it. Just that second of power you have over a child. I knew I couldn't do it again, but I did it several times after words."

"For how long?"

"I stopped when she was fifteen. She moved out at eighteen."

I lay down on Sissy's lap, fighting to keep my eyes open. I felt Sissy's hand stroke my hair. "Don't fight it Mattie. Go to sleep."

I got up the next morning and went right out to the couch. Mom was still facing the back of the couch. "Mommy."

"Let her be," grandma said. I looked up to her and she steered me to the kitchen. Sissy was still in bed.

"Will she come back?"

"Mattie, I know this is hard for you to understand."

"No," I heard from outside the doorway. She is to young to hear this," Shellie came to the door.

"She'll have to find out eventually," grandma said.

"I know," Sissy said looking at me.

About mid-day, mom drug herself off the couch and she left. "Well, she still has a job."

"Maybe. We should check to make sure she is going to work."

Sissy got the stroller and the three of us went for a walk. We went through the park and we saw mommy going through the door of a rundown building.

"That doesn't look like the liquor store."

"It's not," grandma said. "You two stay here."

Grandma disappeared through the door. Sissy looked at me. Grandma came out a few minutes later.

"What happened?" Sissy asked.

"I don't know the lights aren't on. Staying here is too dangerous. Let's wait for her at home."

The three of us waited for four hours at the kitchen table. We played go fish and sat in silence. Mom came through the door and quietly went to her room. Grandma quietly followed her and Sissy held me tight.

"I will not allow this in my house," grandma yelled.

Sissy picked me up and stood in the doorway of the kitchen. Grandma opened the front door and threw something out and closed the door.

That night I wandered into mommy's room and went through her dresser and closet. I found a bag that smelt weird. I picked it up and went to wake up Sissy.

"Sissy," I shook her shoulder. "I found something."

"What Mattie?"

"I found something," I repeated. I showed her the bag. She sat up and grabbed the bag from my hand.

"Where did you get this?" she whispered.

"Mommy's closet."

"Mattie, you know we aren't allowed in there." She got up and came back empty handed. "Don't not go in there again."

"I'm sorry. What's wrong with mommy?"

"Mattie, listen to me. Mommy is going into a dark place and she isn't coming back. We are slowly losing her. She has given up and there's nothing we can do about it."

CHAPTER 8

I am now seven and sissy will be fifteen soon. Mommy was driven to the hospital last night, and grandma never told us why. I lay by Sissy that night, looking up at the ceiling. I didn't want to believe what Sissy was saying about mom, but part of me knew she was right. Grandma came in, turned the light on and woke up Shellie.

"Your mother had a heart attack. She's okay for right now. Do you guys want to see her?"

"No," Sissy said looking at grandma.

"Why not? I want to see her," I said looking at grandma.

"Shellie, come with us. You can stay in the waiting room," grandma suggested.

"Fine," she said sitting up with a huff.

We got to the hospital, and grandma rushed us to mommy's window. She had wires coming out from under her gown. Her eyes were closed and there was a screen showing a green line that was beeping.

"Can we see her?" I asked.

We had to wait a day, so we slept in the waiting room. I was on grandma's lap and fell asleep against her chest. The last ting I heard was her heartbeat.

She woke me and it was light out. I saw a doctor come over to us. He said mom's last name and grandma raised her hand. I woke

Sissy up and followed the doctor to an open door. Grandma put me down and I went over to mommy's hand. "Mommy."

I got nothing. There were fewer wires than last night. I picked my arms up and grandma put me on the bed. I lay on mom's left shoulder. It felt good to lay with her again. "Mommy, mommy, please open your eyes." Her eyes didn't open.

We stayed at the hospital the entire day. I was the only one who never left the room.

"Mattie, we should go home. You haven't had anything to eat today. You didn't drink anything either."

I was feeling a little dizzy. "I want to stay."

"Then please let me get you a drink from the cafeteria."

I went to sleep after grandma and Sissy left the room. I slept all the way through the night. I remember going to sleep with mom's heartbeat. I woke up to her heartbeat faster. I lifted my head. "Mom."

The doctors came in. One gave me to grandma and guided us out of the room. I left with no struggle, and sat in front of the window with my back to mom. Shellie sat next to me and held my hand. I put my head on her shoulder. I starred at the tiles on the floor, and my mind went blank of everything except what life would be like without mom.

It seemed like hours before the doctors came out. "Her heart is very weak."

Grandma looked at us, then back to the doctors. "So are we preparing ourselves for the worse."

"Yes, I'm so sorry."

Judging by the way grandma was talking to the doctor, mom won't be mom for much longer. The doctors let us in, and the wires were back on mom.

"Mommy," I said.

For the first time since she's been in the hospital, her eyes were open. "Mattie."

"Mommy, where are you going?"

"Mommy will never leave you," she said pointing to my chest. "I will always be in here."

Grandma picked me up and put me next to mom. Shellie came to the side of the bed.

"Shellie, I am sorry I wasn't much of a mother to you when Mattie was born. You had grown up sooner than you needed to. You protected your sister in ways I never could have. Thank you."

"Mom, don't say that. You did your job. You protected us. You did!" I could see the tears starting to roll down Sissy's cheeks. "You had other things to worry about. I was the next person in line to take care of Mattie. You did your job mom." Shellie was holding mom's hand and touching mom's hair and face. Mom had a tear forming in the corner of her eye. A doctor came in.

"Mom," mom said. "You are all they have left. Keep your door open to them."

"I have to apologize for everything," grandma said.

"No you don't. Tell me you love me so I can die as if I had a purpose."

"You have fulfilled your purpose as a mother and a daughter. I love you baby. I'll see you soon."

"Mom don't go," Sissy said.

"Shhh baby. It's my time. I have done my fighting." She looked to the doctor. "Can you turn the machines off?"

I laid my head on mom's chest and her heartbeat was slow and steady. I held mom's hand that was on her tummy. "Mom, I'm not ready for this."

The room became quiet as the machines were being turned off. Tears were starting to flow as mom's heartbeat started to slow down. I closed my eyes and squeezed mom's hand. The strong heartbeat that put me to sleep at night was now at rest. Her chest felt hollow. I lifted my head and there were still wet tears on mom's cheeks. Her chest stopped moving and I looked to grandma.

"Will she come back?" I asked.

Shellie picked me up and we sat in the chair, in the corner of the room. I looked at mom, but Shellie turned my head to face her chest.

"Mommy," I said.

CHAPTER 9

It's been a month without mom and everything has gone almost all to hell. Shellie and grandma are arguing constantly. Shellie has been talking about leaving. I've been trying to hide from everything. I went into mom's room and opened the closet door. I found a bag of green stuff. The same bag I found a few years ago. I opened it, smelt it and put my hand in to feel it. I took a pinch of it and put it on my tongue. I spit it back out and heard footsteps. I threw the bag in the closet and closed the door. I got onto the bed and lay on her pillow, but she always slept on the couch, so the pillows still smelt like grandma. I started to tear up and felt a presence at the door. I kept still and my eyes closed.

"Mattie." I opened my eyes and looked to grandma. "Why in the floor green?"

"I wanted to try it."

"Try what?"

"The stuff in mommy's closet."

Grandma opened the closet and bag I had opened was now on the carpet. "No, bad. Don't you ever touch this stuff again."

"Why is it still in here?" Sissy said from the door. "Mom has been gone a month. She doesn't use it anymore."

"I never got around to cleaning it out."

"Why not? You're never busy."

"Well, I had to get you guys moved in a settled."

"We've been here for four years," Sissy yelled.

"Maybe four years is one year to many."

"Are you kicking us out?"

"I would certainly like to, but I promised your mother I would keep an open door."

"Some promises are meant to be broken." Sissy stormed out of the room and slammed the door.

"I'm sorry grandma," I said.

She turned away and left the room. Shellie eventually came back in. "Mattie we have to leave. One of us is going to get hurt."

"You mean you're going to get hurt?"

"Yes, but I will protect you anyway I can."

"So, when do you want to leave?"

"Soon," she said. "Pack your things tonight."

The rest of the night was quiet. Dinner was awkward, but Sissy was really good at being mom. She would tuck me in at night and wash away the bad dreams.

I went to sleep, about a week after Sissy suggested we leave, with Sissy beside me, and when I woke up half way through the night I was in the stroller. It was still dark out.

"Sissy?"

"Mattie, did you have everything?"

"Yes Sissy."

I was holding the doggie mommy had got for me, and the teddy bear Shellie had gotten for me on my second birthday. I knew Sissy was wearing mom's necklace.

"Where are we going?" I asked.

"I'll figure something out. Go back to sleep."

I woke up on a mattress with Sissy next to me. I sat up and looked around. It looked like an abandoned something. I got up and started exploring.

"Mattie," I heard a little while after I left Sissy's side.

"Shellie, I'm okay. Where are we?"

"Come here, and I will tell you."

Sissy was still on the mattress. "Do you recognize this place at all?"

"No."

"Are you sure? We put it up for sale and it never sold. This is our house."

I started looking around and saw a familiar hallway. I remember running in this hallway, away from mommy. I could feel the tickle on my tummy. Then I heard dad's voice.

"Why did we come here?"

"It's the only place I could think of," she said.

"Good choice." I walked over to her. "So what now?"

"Don't know. We don't have anyone else to turn to. We can always make do here. I'll see what I can do about money, but we will have to make do."

"Grandma's door is still open?"

"I don't think she will ever welcome us back there."

Shellie and I were on the brink of starvation. We were able to get water from the neighbors. There was one day I went to get water with Shellie and the neighbors offered us food as well. They were nice people, but there were nights when their arguing kept me up.

Sissy got a job at the food store as a shelf organizer. She fills the shelves when they get empty. I was alone a lot more now. I was really exploring the house now. I was looking everywhere for good memories and bad. My room was the only place I had good memories. All the furniture was still there, just over grown with weeds and moss.

Sissy would leave at nine in the morning and come home around three or four. She told me five at the latest. It was now five-thirty, and still no Sissy. I was getting cold, worried and lonely. There were no lights and I was feeling claustrophobic.

"Sissy," I said every time I heard a noise. I found the mattress and my doggie and teddy bear.

"Mattie, I'm so sorry I'm late baby. My boss kept me until the next shift came in. You okay?"

"Just scared."

"I'm coming hold on."

I laid down knowing I will soon be safe in Shellie's arms. Sleep came right as Sissy sat on the bed.

It took us six months to get out of the rundown house. We found a cheap apartment, and Sissy got a second job. She was off on Sundays. That was the only day we got together, and she always slept until noon. I was really starting to miss the days when we spent every moment together.

The good thing about life being just Shellie and I was we spent holidays, birthdays and eventually weekends together. Sissy turned sixteen last month and I would be turning nine in October. Her life was becoming busy and sometimes it felt like time with me didn't matter anymore.

"Sissy, what happened to the time we had before?"

"Mattie, I need these jobs to get us money. If I didn't have a job we would still be at the house."

"I miss you Shellie."

"Trust me Mattie I miss you too, but this is for the better."

CHAPTER 10

I was still alone the same amount of time as last year, but at least the apartment has light and heat.

Shellie was now doing the afternoon shift at the store, but doing mornings at a different store, so now she is gone from eight in the morning to eight at night. In the summer time that's fine, but in the winter it's dark at four-thirty. I have four hours of dark in an apartment with my doggie and teddy. There are times I cry myself to sleep before Shellie gets home. She usually wakes me up to let me know she's home and to reassure me that I'm not alone anymore. I feel her get into bed beside me. I pretend to sleep, but I love when she puts her arm over me. It gives me the sense of security that mom used to give me.

I always wake up before her and look down at her. She seems to look more tired every day. It was Saturday, so I knew she didn't have to work today. She got up around noon and came out in the living room with a smile on her face. She ran over to me, picked me up and hugged me tight.

"Shellie, did something good happen?"

"No, I just have off today."

"What are we doing then?"

"Well, it's cold. It can be a movie day. Go pick out movies. I don't care which."

I ran into our room, so excited to finally spend time with my sister. I grabbed a whole bunch of movies not knowing what I grabbed, and went back out to the TV. I put the first movie in and went to the kitchen. Shellie was making brunch and was in a strangely good mood.

"You sure everything is okay?"

"Yes Mattie, stop asking." Her mood suddenly changed. I left her alone and saw my movie was starting.

We watched movies all day. We didn't bother to turn the lights on when it got dark. It was better dark. It made it feel more like a movie theatre.

We were on our seventh movie at least, it was six o'clock and Sissy and I were lying down. Her one arm was under me while the other one was over me. I giggled at one part and looked back at Shellie. She was asleep. I smiled and cuddle closer to her.

I woke up half way through the night, and the TV was still on. I was still in the living room, and for the first time ever Shellie was not beside me.

"Shellie," I yelled. I walked throughout the apartment and found Sissy out cold on the bed. I turned the side lamp on, and on the bed near Sissy's hand was a needle. I looked down at Shellie and touched her hair. I had a good idea of what it was. I sat on the bed next to her, and her eyes opened half way.

"Shellie, you left me."

"Mattie," she said tearing up. "I don't want to lie to you."

"So don't, tell me the truth."

"I can't tell you the truth either."

"I'm old enough. I have the right to know."

The room went silent and I looked at Shellie. Her eyes rolled back and she became unresponsive. I climbed on top of her and tried to calm her down, but this wasn't a panic attack. Grandma called it a seizure.

"Sissy, it's Mattie. Talk to me Shellie."

As fast as it came, the seizure left. I left the room and went downstairs. I asked for a computer and researched seizure and drugs, and found that what my sister was injecting into her body was crack.

Sissy didn't go to work the next morning. She said she called out.

"I want to go to the hockey game today," I said. "It's free."

"So go," she said.

"Will you let me go alone?"

"Do whatever you want."

"No, I want you to come with me."

"I don't want to."

"Shellie, I lost my mother to drugs. I don't plan on losing my sister to them too." I went over to her and took the bag from her hand. "Please come with me."

She became submissive and got up.

The arena was within walking distance. I carried Shellie's purse and we found good seats, kind of in the middle.

On the way home from the game Shellie was holding my hand. When we got out of the crowd she dropped my hand. As soon as she let go of my hand she was pulled backward. The man holding Sissy looked oddly familiar. I remember him very faintly in my memories.

"Shellie," the man said.

"Dad."

"Dad," I repeated.

"Mattie, go home," she yelled.

"I don't know how."

"Yes you do, go."

"This must be Mattie," dad said.

"Leave her alone," Shellie said. "Mattie, go home."

"Will you come back?"

"I don't know. Go home now." I started walking backward and dad threw Shellie to the ground. "Mattie run!"

I didn't question anything. I turned and ran. His footsteps came louder, then stopped. I slowed and turned around. Dad was dragging Shellie the opposite way. I wanted to follow them, but Shellie told me to go home. Maybe I should disobey her this one time?

I stood on the sidewalk looking which way to go. It was starting to get cold, so I went home. The end of the month was coming, so rent was due soon. I had two weeks to figure what I was going to do next.

CHAPTER 11

The apartment kept me two months after the last rent was paid, then asked me to leave because I wasn't paying rent. I haven't heard anything from Shellie, grandma or dad. I was truly alone now. It was just me now. My rolling backpack followed me and some of Shellie's stuff came along. I was holding my mom's doggie and Sissy's teddy bear, and kept my eyes on the sidewalk. I did bring a bag of the stuff that I found in mom's closet, and the white powder in the bag I found with Sissy that one night.

The days always felt to short in the fall season. The sun was setting again, all to soon. I needed to find a place to stay.

There was a rundown basement that felt heated. I went in and there was one night light on. At least I was protected from the elements. I dropped my backpack handle and the bag made a thud sound on the concrete floor. I looked around in Shellie's purse, near the night light and found a flashlight. I shined the light beam around and the basement didn't look half bad. There was a mattress on a bed frame. The bed had a blanket on it. The walls were brick with small openings where bricks used to be. I got comfy on the bed and felt very alone without Shellie holding me. Sleep came with no problems.

I could see Shellie being taken from my grasp. I could see dad's face looking at me the way he did when he was holding Shellie. My eyes shot open and I could hear my sister's voice. I looked beside me, but the bed was empty. I sat up, grabbed my stuffed animals, my bag and the green bag from mom's closet, and left.

I walked down the dark street with dim streetlights. They gave off an amber light, making the street look very eerie. I walked for what seemed like forever, and then I heard music. I walked until I was standing in a large warehouse doorway. There were people there of all ages, even kids that were my age. I went in and was suddenly lost. I didn't know which way to go. Someone came over to me and pointed me in the right direction.

"What is this place?"

"A place you will never forget."

The kids welcomed me and took the bag of green from my hand. "We have a newbie tonight."

I looked around and saw one kid open the bag I brought, roll it in paper and come over to me. He held it out. "Try it. You won't regret it."

I took it from him, he lit the end and I took a breath in. I coughed it back out.

"It's all good. We all start out rough," the boy said. "Name's Rob."

"Mattie," I said.

"Try it again."

I sucked in again and it wasn't so bad. I still coughed a little, but it was good. As I was finishing a girl was rolling me another one.

"So how did you guys end up here?"

"We live here," Rob said. "We smoke twice a week for the whole year then we switch drugs."

The word drugs brought me to back to the white powder I found near my sister. "What is this?"

"Marijuana."

"Would I be able to join you guys? I just lost my sister and I hate being alone."

"I don't see why not," he said handing me another one.

"How long have you been doing this?"

"Which one? Smoking or the gathering?"

"Well, both," I said.

"The gathering started when the first homeless kid found out about drugs."

"Where is Homeless kid now?"

"He's the one that pointed you towards us," Rob said pointing to the lone teenager by the door.

"So if all we are is homeless, then why are we smoking like this?" I asked putting my pot down.

"The drugs became his escape. He didn't force us, we tried it out at our own will."

"And now…"

"And now we can go to our happy place and forget about the fact that we don't belong anywhere."

"I belong with my sister," I said.

"Where is she?"

"She was kidnapped."

"So you're alone?"

"Yes I'm alone," I said looking down to my pot and lifting it back to my lips.

I cannot tell you how many rolls Rob had given me, but it gave me a sensation that my mom never gave me. I was laying on the floor smoking what I say is my last one for the night and mom came into my thoughts, so did Shellie.

"What are you doing?" mom said.

"Grandma told you bad," Shellie said. "Why did you take it? You should be staying alive, looking for me."

I was suddenly full of guilt. Rob handed me another one. I looked at it and stuck it in my mouth. He lit it for me. This high is allowing me to hear mom and Shellie again. I will be with Rob every week.

CHAPTER 12

I was doing pot on my own when I wasn't with Rob, for the past year. I was living between by myself and with Rob and his group. Anytime I was with Rob they would get me high as the sky. Mom and Shellie would then yell at me. I didn't like it when they yelled, but I liked hearing their voices. I eventually decided to live permanently with Rob and his friends. I was now getting high every night, but was still attached to my doggie from mom and still attached to my thoughts with mom and Shellie. The real world didn't seem real anymore.

At night I found myself going to sleep with a pot roll in one hand and Rob's hand in the other. I was beginning to feel safe again. The voices of mom and Shellie were slowly fading. My doggie was spending more time with my bag, and I was spending more time in a high that didn't exist.

There came a two-week span of no drugs, and three days in my body didn't like the fact of not getting the drug. Rob never left my side, even though he was going through the same event as I was.

"What is this?" I asked.

"You are going through withdrawal," he said. "My body is some what used to it, that's why I am not as bad."

"Why aren't we smoking today?"

"Homeless kid has something else for us to try. He puts us through withdrawal, so as to not overwhelm the body with different drugs at the same time. This is almost like a rest period for us. It sucks, but it's worth it."

"What drug did he get for us to try?"

"Cocaine."

My mind went back to what I found out about cocaine. I did not want to try it. I saw what it was doing to my sister, and I'm sure she would yell at me for it.

"What's that?"

"Well, on the streets we call it crack."

"My sister used it before we got split up. I don't know if I want to do it."

"You want to remember your past. Do you want to remember the look on your sister's face when she was kidnapped? If you don't then try this stuff."

"Hey, you said that I try this stuff on my own. It sounds like you are pressuring me."

"Not pressure, just trying to rid you of your pain," he said.

"Maybe when I am better, I should leave. I can hear my mom and sister yelling at me."

"You want to be alone. We took you in, gave you food. You were on the brink of dying."

"I know, but mom always told me drugs were bad." I said looking away.

"Your mom isn't here to tell you no. Do you remember that high you had? Everything went away. Everything became easy."

"It did. I liked it."

"So let's go another year. When you turn fourteen we'll introduce you to drinking."

"Am I the youngest one here?"

"Yeah, but we will get a new youngster soon. Age doesn't matter here." He held something in his hand. Through blurred vision I saw him hand me another joint.

"Is it safe for me to have this right now?"

"Yeah, you'll get a small high and your body will remember it."

Rob sat me up then lit the joint. I sucked in and my heart began to race, then mom and Shellie disappeared from my thoughts.

"We should be starting the new drug in the next few days. Try to get some sleep."

Rob lay down then slowly laid me down next to him. I finished my joint, held Rob's hand and went to sleep.

I could see Shellie being dragged down the sidewalk, and the sound of a heartbeat started and came to a stop. I was back in the hospital with mom, and all the pain came back. I heard a long beep and sat straight up. My shirt was soaked and Rob was facing away from me. I couldn't change my shirt because I didn't know where my bag was, and I was in a room with people I have just met. "Rob," I said. "Rob, I need help."

"Mattie," he said tired. "What is it? Are you okay?"

"Where's my bag? I have to change my shirt. I had a bad dream."

"Oh, here." He handed me a flashlight.

"I don't know where it is though."

He got up and brought my bag over. I turned the light off, changed my shirt and lay back down. Sleep never came again that night, but Rob had his arm around me the rest of the night.

CHAPTER 13

My twelfth birthday, like every other birthday I have had became just another day in the year. They didn't really matter anymore. I decided to look in a mirror that I had been avoiding for months. My eyes were bloodshot from the marijuana, and now my body was changing because I'm putting cocaine into the mix now too. Rob was showing me how to self-inject the drug right into my bloodstream. He had to do it for me the first few times. When I finally did it myself it felt good. He had laid the cocaine in a line on the table and breathed in through his nose. To me it looked like it would be wonderful, but I didn't want it to hurt.

It was now six months into the new drug. The group hasn't slept in three nights, myself included. We've been playing games those three nights and then injecting ourselves during the day. I am trying so hard to fight the want. I know I need to cut back, and for some reason I am hearing mom and Shellie again. The guilt is coming back and I am forcing myself to cut back, but Rob always comes over with another needle full or lays powder in front of me, and I just cant help myself.

"I can't keep up with you guys," I said to Rob when he came over with another needle.

"What are you talking about?"

"You guys have been doing this for four years right?"

"This is only my second year, well my first year on cocaine. I don't want it. I can hear my mom again."

He put the needle on the table and left. I starred at the needle, and no one came over to me. I still had a good high. I had energy to burn. I know I didn't need that needle. *I don't need it.*

An hour went by and I had gotten up, leaving the needle on the table. I found Rob in the crowd and joined them. About a half hour later I could feel my energy level drop. I felt tired, but I could not pick up that needle. I went to my mattress and sat down. I knew if I sat down I wouldn't want to get back up. I looked at the other kids having fun, and injecting themselves with more of the drug. I was starting to feel the want more then ever right now. I looked back over to the table. I lay down and looked to the ceiling. My body and mind were telling me to get it, but my heart was saying stop, to leave, to find Shellie.

Rob came over. "What are you doing?"

"Laying down, forcing myself to say no to the drug."

"How long have you gone without it?"

"About two hours."

"Your feeling like this because you last injection has worn off. Let me get you another."

"I don't want one," I yelled.

"Just because your hearing voices in your head doesn't mean you have to take your problems out on me," he shot back.

"I'm not taking anything out on anyone. I'm confused, lost, hurt and now high. My life is a wreck. I don't know what I'm doing. Your telling me one thing while my mom and sister are telling me something else."

"Then stop listening to everyone else and do what you think you need to do."

I quickly got up and went over to the table and stuck the needle in my arm. The rush came back and my tiredness went away. I re-joined the group and another night went by.

The sun came through the small windows of the warehouse door and everyone has crashed except me. Well, I was tired but sleep never came for me. Rob kid of tossed and turned all night.

My sleep came later on in the day and of course my dream of Shellie being taken from me came back, followed by the stopping of my mother's heart. Then my mom's voice talked to me giving me her words of wisdom that didn't really matter to me anymore, *Mattie, you need to stop this. This is not how I want you to spend your life. You are taking years off your life. Don't make my mistake Mattie.* I woke with a jump when I heard Shellie scream. Rob was next to me still asleep. I wondered what time it was, and I felt really hungry. Homeless kid came over to me and handed me a needle.

"I don't want it."

"Why not?"

"I'm starting to feel normal again."

"You had a nightmare of your mom."

"Yes, that's because I was with her when she died."

"So you will forget that when you have this."

"I don't want to forget it," I said starting to tear up.

I felt Rob move behind me. "Let me talk to her."

I turned to face Rob and Homeless kid walked away. "I really don't want to forget my mom."

"He meant to say that you would only forget the time of her death."

"That's what I mean Rob. That is something I don't want to forget."

"When you got here you said that that was what you wanted to forget?" he said confused.

"That was a year ago. Things change."

"It's your choice. Like I said we won't force you to do anything."

Some of the kids had restarted the drug. Rob was back to sleep and I never left his side. I put my head on his chest and could finally hear another heartbeat. It was so wonderful. I could feel something inside me started to feel something more for him. He is almost become like a father I never had, but maybe more like a brother. I relaxed my head on his chest and everything happened at once. His body started to shake and he was having a nightmare. I sat up and felt Homeless kid standing behind me.

"Talk to him," he said.

"How?"

"You'll figure it out," he said then walked away.

"Rob, it's my turn to help you now. You have so much locked up inside. Maybe if you talked about it, you wouldn't need the drugs anymore. Please fight through this and come back to me. Open your eyes and I'll be right here."

I waited and his eyes eventually opened.

"You okay?" I asked.

"I saw my family."

"Rob what happened?"

"A fire happened."

"Tell me," I said touching his hand.

"It happened so fast we didn't have enough time to get out. My parents left. My brother got me out. He had third degree burns all over him and had passed on in the hospital. That happened when I was ten."

"Where did your parents go?"

He sat up. "Dad left then mom decided she couldn't do it herself, so she left. My brother became dad and my protector."

He rolled up his sleeve and pant's leg and pulled up his shirt. His whole left side was scarred, but not his face.

"You know, you would never know by looking at you that you ever had a scar like that. I still like you for you."

"Thank you Mattie."

"Open up more often. It'll make you feel better," I smiled. He sat up and walked to the door. It looked cold outside. I'm very happy I stayed.

Rob and I were still doing drugs because we missed the instant rush of the cocaine, but we were able to fight the want a little harder. On our down time we told each other the stuff in the past that we were trying to forget.

It was weird when he wished me happy birthday, although I do remember telling him that. This was my first party since I was four. The party involved drugs and alcohol, but it's my new lifestyle, so I cut loose that night.

The next morning everything hurt and the room was spinning now more than the night before. I realized I had gotten drunk at the age of thirteen. I know my mom had raised me better than this, but the drugs were beginning to take their hold. A hold I can never break.

CHAPTER 14

We continued to use marijuana and crack while homeless kid was rotating drugs for another year. Rob had said something about ecstasy. I was now becoming curious about new drugs, but I had to wait three more days.

The final day before the new drug the whole group got completely wasted. I was very close, but I still remember the occasion. I was able to fight my want and just had a few drinks. Rob on the other hand was drinking along with the pot and crack, and by two in the afternoon he was so beyond wrecked. I was telling him to stop, but he didn't who I was. The time came when Homeless kid stepped in and gave Rob something to knock him out. I had tears in my eyes when I walked to Rob's side. I touched his back and rolled him over. That's when I got scared. That's when I realized that I could die tomorrow from this stuff.

I opened my eyes the next morning and it felt like the room was spinning. I sat up, and that just made it worse. My feet were now on the concrete floor, and it was me that was spinning. I heard footsteps come over and a hand on my shoulder. I looked up and saw Homeless kid through the blurred vision. He handed me something. It looked like the ecstasy pills. It sounded like the pills too. I could feel homeless kid lay me back down.

"Sleep it off," he said.

I put my hand on Rob's shoulder and easily went to sleep.

I could see Shellie and see where dad might have brought her. I knew if I was ever going to help her I had to break the grasp of the drugs. She was saying *don't hurt me* over and over again. I was wondering what he was doing to her. She screamed and I woke up.

Homeless kid was right I do feel better. The pills were the first things I saw when I sat up.

"Dammit," I said opening the pack.

"No," I heard from behind me. "You, you have to wait until the party tonight."

"What party?"

"You'll see," he smirked and walked away.

I was on my mattress watching Homeless kid hand out pills to everyone. I laid down trying to recover from last night. Rob said that we were going out tonight.

"Where, it's cold out."

"Yeah well it's cold every time we do this drug. I'll keep you warm. Come on."

I put my hoodie on and realized I hadn't changed my clothes in god knows how many days, and I didn't really care.

"Where are we going?"

"When was the last time you felt clean?"

"I don't remember. Where are we going for showers though? Everything costs money."

"Trust us. The showers work."

"Rob, why can't you just tell me?"

"I don't want to," he yelled.

I gave cleanish clothes to Homeless kid and we left.

It felt good to not be greasy anymore. It was about four-thirty now, and the sun was just starting to set. For once I wanted to be outside, but I wasn't alone. I brought a few joints out with me. I was looking at the sky through the strands of my hair.

Ever since I got here, since mom and Shellie yelled at me through my dreams, I felt safe behind my hair. My hair hides the monster that I have become. Maybe if I hide the monster, the innocent girl I once was will come back. As I am thinking this, I am lighting another joint for my body to take in, and for my body to make me pay for it later on. Honestly, I couldn't care less about what my body wants and doesn't want.

I've been looking in the mirror more often now, just wondering what I look like to the other kids. I've lost weight, which is scary because I didn't have much weight to begin with. I look older than fourteen and my eyes look hollow. My grasp on the outside world is gone and my connection with mom and Shellie has been broken.

"Mattie."

I was still in front of the mirror. "What?"

"It's time for the love drug to do its job."

"The love drug?"

"It's another way of saying ecstasy. The best way is to take ecstasy is in a party environment."

"Oh, well why didn't you say that before. Let's party."

"I didn't want to," he yelled and walked away.

I looked back into the mirror and zoned out again.

The party has started and I've started the new drug. After a while the music started to blur together, but it was the high that I wanted to keep. I could see the blurry outlines of the colored lights blending together. I was dancing with everyone, but mostly Rob. Even though he was high too, I felt safe with him. I felt even safer when I felt his hands on my hips. It felt as if the party lasted all night, but only about four hours went by before kids started dropping where they stood. The music went off and normal lights came on. I was sweating more now then ever before in my life. Everything was blurred more now than it was before. I could see where Rob was.

"Rob oh my gosh. This is better than pot and crack together."

I hear something fall and looked through my blurry eyes and Rob had fallen like the other kids. I slowly got to my knees and felt my stomach churning. I heard and garbage can put beside me, and a hand on my head. I assumed it was Homeless kid.

"You're okay. It will pass."

I was able to throw up and looked to Homeless kid, then back to Rob.

"Can I stop?"

"Why would you want to do that?" he asked.

"I know I am better than this."

"Are you forgetting your past?"

"Yes I am, but I see and hear my sister and my mom in my dreams. They are yelling at me because they know I am better than this."

"It doesn't matter what they say. What do you want?"

"I want another round of ecstasy," I said.

CHAPTER 15

My body became so used to the ecstasy that I had forgotten all about the marijuana. We had a party twice a week, and the other days of the week were for us to recover and have other drugs. I've been fourteen now for six months or so. I don't want to get rid of the drugs anymore. They have become part of who I am. We will be switching to a new drug soon and honestly I can't wait.

It was a party night and Rob and I were dancing on the balcony. I hadn't eaten anything for the last two days. Homeless kid would walk around and make sure everyone had what we needed. Kids were still dropping from dehydration and exhaustion. My vision was blurry and I'm starting to not remember the way the night started, or how I got to this point in time. I know I am talking but I can't hear myself. Through my blurry eyes I saw someone come up to me, then everything became out of control. I was in a fistfight with some random girl. I didn't know if she was high or not, but damn could she throw a punch. The blurry vision went away and everything went dark.

When I opened my eyes, Rob and Homeless kid were beside me. I could only open one eye and my whole body ached. "What happened?"

"You don't remember?"

"I was as high as high could get. How long was I out for?"

"You were out for about an hour. You some how started talking to one of the toughest chicks here. You didn't know what you were saying, but you couldn't have said anything worse. It's weird because ecstasy makes you happy and everyone around you happy. I don't think she was high though."

"What did I do?"

"You don't know anything about her, but some how you found out her information and started spilling it out to her face. I tried to tell her you were really high but she threw me to the side and used you for punching practice. It took three of the big guys to get her off you," Rob explained.

"Do you have a mirror?"

"Mattie, I really don't think you want to see yourself. You're pretty banged up. You need rest."

"I need the drug," I said.

"You will get it when you are healed," Homeless kid said.

"I want it now," I yelled.

"She's in a lot of pain. I have the drug in stock. It's a pain killer," Homeless kid said.

"Is it okay for her to have it after getting off such a good high?"

"I guess we will have to see?"

"I can't let you give it to her if you don't what will happen."

"Give me the drug," I said.

"Mattie, listen to me," Rob said. "I need to give you a day rest before we give you the new drug. We don't know how your body will react to such a quick switch."

Rob sat by my head with a joint in his hand. I laid on the floor silent, oblivious to what was around me. I was tired and kept seeing mom. I starred at the ceiling and my dream became almost real. I could see Shellie. She was screaming and looked so weak.

"Shellie," I said reaching my hand up to grab hers.

"Mattie, it's okay. Whatever you are seeing right now, it isn't real."

I felt Rob's hand put my arm back to the ground. I could feel myself start to tear up. I didn't fight any of it. I let the vision take me where it wanted to go. The pain became too great and sleep took me.

"Leave her alone," someone yelled and yanked me out of sleep. My eyes shot open and Rob was standing in front of a girl. I sat up.

"Is this her?" I asked.

"Yes," Rob said.

Homeless kid came over and calmed the girl down.

"I'm sorry," I said. "I was so high I didn't know what I was doing. I am sorry that I offended you the way I did. I don't remember what I said, and I will never do it again. It was not my place to speak out about a complete stranger."

I lay back down and touched my eye. Homeless kid came over with something in his hand. I saw which way he came from. "You remember me saying about the pain killer. I am going to put it right here by Rob so he can give it to you tomorrow."

After he left I knew where to get those pills. There has got to be a supply somewhere around here. I saw a door on the far side of the warehouse, and knew that, that was where he had to be keeping these pills.

Everyone was asleep, and I took the flash light from the other side of Rob. He whispered my name and I looked down at him. His eyes were still closed. I got up and slowly walked to the "pill room." This was the first time, since I was here, that I was roaming around in the dark. There were kids randomly placed on the floor. I moved slowly, but swiftly. I passed Homeless kid, asleep on his own mattress, and made it to the door. I quietly turned the knob and it opened. I shined the flashlight up and there were shelves with boxes upon boxes of everything. I didn't know where to start looking and I was feeling tired again.

"He did say the name of the pill," I whispered to myself. "Opium."

I started looking around for the name. There were several boxes with the name on it. One of the boxes was open. I grabbed what I could and made hammock with my shirt. I went back to the door and started closing it, but it squeaked, so I just left it open. I found my bag and put my stash inside, then went back to Rob. I lie on his arm and almost fell asleep instantly.

I slept the rest of the night and had nightmares of Shellie and what dad was doing or has done to her. She would be twenty-one by now. Maybe she got out and was looking for me. Maybe I'm talking crazy and Shellie was dead.

Rob woke me up. My eye was a little more open today. Rob had an ice pack in his hand and reached toward my bag. I had butterflies in my tummy, as his hand got closer, and sighed in relief when just a shirt came out.

"You okay?" he asked. "You're looking a little pale."

"I'm okay," I said as he put the ice to my eye.

I saw Homeless kid come over. "Did you take my pills?"

"No," I said trying to lie. He went over to my bag.

"No," he said as he lifted the pills in his hands.

"I'm sorry. I am, but I need them. You can't take away what an addict wants."

"Oh yeah, watch me," he said walking away.

I could feel the tears starting to come. My eyes filled up. Rob looked down at me. "You took his pills?"

"Yeah last night?"

"Wow, I'm, uh, I'm impressed. I've been wanting to do that for years."

"Why haven't you?" I asked.

"Never had the courage to do it," he smiled.

I smiled back. "What if we take a few pills and leave, just the two of us? I have to find my sister. You can live with us."

"I don't know," he said. "This has been my home for so long."

"Maybe you need to leave. We can get better and can finally have a normal life."

"Where will we stay? It's very cold out right now."

"We will manage. I have managed for three years here. C'mon you're not going to make me do this alone. Are you?"

"No, you're not going to do it alone. We will leave in the very early morning. Get your rest now." He lay down next to me. To my surprise Homeless kid came back over with a pill in hand.

"If you ever steal from me again you will never..."

"Relax, besides what can you do to me that won't get you in trouble with the police."

He looked very upset, and mad after I said that. He left and Rob looked at me. "That's no way to say you're sorry. You are digging yourself into a deeper hole. Stop being a jerk and get some sleep."

"Okay," I giggled. He kissed my forehead and held me closer.

I woke up in a dark room. I had slept until night came. Rob was asleep next to me. I did wonder what time it was. I went over to my bag to see if any of the pills were left behind. There was. I took one and the pain in my eye instantly went away.

"Mattie."

I went back over to Rob.

"I'm right here," I said.

"It's two in the morning. We should go. We will find another place to sleep. I have a fair share of stuff in my pocket. Let's go."

"I only have enough opium for a week or two. I need more."

"Hey," he whispered. "You said you want to get better. Leave with what you have."

"I don't want to go through the withdrawal stage again."

"Well, to get better you are going to have to. C'mon," he said leading me toward the door. We slightly and quickly opened the door, and the cold air hit me like a ton of bricks.

"I know of a heated building over there," he pointed.

"It seems far."

"The faster we go, the faster we will be warm again."

My eye and head were starting to bother me again, but I forced myself to wait until we got to the shelter.

Rob was carrying me when I woke up. "Where is my bag?"

"I have it," he said.

"What happened?"

"You had a seizure. It's a withdrawal symptom from the marijuana and crack you haven't had in a few weeks."

He stopped walking, knelt down and looked at me. "You do understand that once you run out of opium your body will back fire. You're not getting the drugs anymore, so your body will have to adjust to its old ways."

"I understand."

CHAPTER 16

We got to the building in less time that I was expecting. Rob insisted he carry me the whole way, so I let him.

When we got inside and settled, I had another pill and Rob had another joint. "The faster we finish, the faster we can get through the withdrawal stage."

I finally looked in a mirror and saw my eye, and it was getting better, but still looked bad.

I was now fifteen. It's only been a few days since we left the group. I knew that I needed to rest but I needed to start to look for Shellie. "Rob, I need to find my sister."

"I promise, we will start the search tomorrow. We should get back to sleep."

I had forgotten that it was still dark. He laid me down and forced me to relax. The opium finally kicked in and sleep came fast.

I could see Shellie. She was looking for me, but dad was looking for her. She has been running for a few months now, trying not to let him find her.

I woke with a jump and it was light outside. I looked up to Rob and he was still asleep. I slowly got up and went outside. The sun was hitting the most perfect spot. I took a joint from Rob's stuff and a lighter, and then went outside. The sun made it feel twenty degrees warmer that what it really was.

"Mattie," I heard from inside. I didn't budge. I wanted to finish my joint, and I didn't want to move. "Mattie."

"Uh," I said getting up. "What Rob? I'm outside."

"Sorry, I got worried."

He came out with a joint and sat next to me. "When we leaving?"

"I think we should stay. If she is looking for me, then I feel I should just stay put."

"What if dad finds you first?"

"He won't."

"What if…"

"He won't. Shellie will find me," I said looking down the road where we came from last night.

It's been a week since my last pill and like Rob said, my body was starting to back fire. I wished, more than anything that my sister was here.

"Mattie," I heard her say. I was in and out of sleep and the seizures were taking over. I felt most relaxed at night, but I wake up sweating and going back to sleep with the chills. "Mattie."

"Mattie, hey," I hear Rob say. "We have a visitor."

I opened my eyes and he helped me sit up.

"Mattie," she said excited. "Mattie, oh my gosh, what happened to you."

"I was trying to find a way to escape the loss of you and mom." I stopped talking and tried to fight sleep.

"It's okay Mattie, it's okay. Go to sleep. We are safe. I'll be here when you wake up."

"Shellie," I said drifting off.

I woke up and night had fallen. I sat up and was once again drenched in sweat. I grabbed a sweatshirt and headed towards the door. My eyes still felt heavy as I walked to the exit. I put my hand on the door and fell to my knees. My vision blurred as the hot flash came and left just as quick. I was able to open the door and crawled outside. I left the door open behind me. I found stairs to the roof, and slowly got to my feet. I stumbled into the wall, and made my way up the stairs. The last few steps were the hardest. My feet were feeling like bricks. I got to the flat roof and walked to the edge. My sister and Rob were not as strong as the drugs. The drugs were screaming *JUMP*, but my sister would say *FIGHT IT*.

I was standing at the edge looking down at the ground. It seemed so much higher than being on the ground looking up.

"Shellie." I closed my eyes. I nearly lost my balance, and then took a step back. "Shellie."

"Mattie, where are you?"

I could see her from the roof. "Shellie."

She looked up. "Rob, get up. Come help me."

Shellie started climbing the stairs and Rob was a little ways behind her. When she got to the roof she slowed, and held her hand out.

"Mattie let us help you. We promise, from here it will not get worse. Every thing from here will only get better. I will not break that promise. Now let's get back down on the ground."

"You promised me you wouldn't leave me. You made that promise when I was two."

"I know Mattie. I know I broke that promise, but I came back. Both times I came back."

The heaviness in my eyes took over and my legs collapsed beneath me.

"Mattie," I heard.

We were back inside when I woke up. "I'm sorry."

"Mattie, it was the drugs. No need to be sorry baby. You are safe now. You need to take it easy, and from now on you are sleeping between us.'

"Okay," I smiled.

I was sleeping on and off for a week, then heard footsteps outside our door. Shellie got us all into hiding. We got behind and within crates. I lay on Rob and tried to keep calm. As soon as the person talked I knew who it was. Shellie looked at Rob. "Who are you calling?"

"The police," he whispered.

The footsteps came in and started walking around. My eyes were feeling heavy again, but I couldn't sleep at a time like this, I talk in my sleep, especially right now.

"Rob," Shellie whispered. "Keep her awake."

"I'm trying," I mouthed.

She put her hand on my cheek. "I'm not going to let anything happen to you."

She put her finger to her lips. Rob held me tighter and I rested my head on is forearm. I was telling myself to stay awake, but sleep took me.

"Mattie," Rob whispered. "Stay awake for me."

I could still hear footsteps.

"Sorry," I whispered. "I can't."

"Just a little longer," Shellie said.

The footsteps stopped close to us. I looked at Shellie and saw tears on her cheeks. Her grip on my hand was turning my fingertips purple.

The footsteps left and Shellie stuck her head out, and then sat back down in relief.

"Hello, police," we heard from the door.

Shellie went out to see the police. "You okay?"

"A man just left. He shouldn't be to far ahead. He held me prisoner for five years. He drugged me and touched me. That man used to be my father. He wants my sister. Please find him and put him behind bars."

I heard a male voice and sat up. I could see the policeman through a hole in the crates and he was holding up and picture. It was a picture of my father. The police left a little while later after asking a few questions. I was able to drift back off and was grateful for a dreamless sleep.

Night came, but for once I was the one who couldn't sleep. Even though I was between Shellie and Rob, the chills that ran though my body took my breath away. I sat up and pulled the blanket up.

"Shellie."

"Mattie, what is it?"

"I'm cold."

She felt my skin. "You are burning up baby. Let's get some layers off of you."

She took my sweatshirt off, and my shirt. That left me with an undershirt and sweat pants. My breathing started to speed up as she laid me back down. She put an arm under my head and Rob woke up. He rolled over to face me and gave me his warmth.

"Everything we went through was worth it. We found each other. We are both alive and dad will never hurt us again. For right now I need you to sleep."

She put my head against her chest and I heard her heartbeat. For so long it had been the drugs putting me to sleep.

CHAPTER 17

I was now sixteen, and was recovering from withdrawal, as was Rob. We were still in the same building, and I had a feeling that dad was still out there looking for me.

Shellie had laid me down next to Rob. He was asleep. He was getting over his seizures, and body temperature changes. I was still fighting with my seizures. Shellie would talk to me, and I would try to talk back. She would put her finger to my lips. She always let me drift off after words.

I had just woken up to a quiet surrounding. Shellie wasn't next to me. I looked to the doorway and she was walking over. "We need to hide."

I woke Rob up and we got in and within the crates. It was now my turn to hold Rob. It was the same voice.

"Hello. I know you are in here," the voice said.

I asked Rob where his phone was. He said it was out by the beds. We never cleaned up our stuff, and my doggie from mom was out there.

"He knows we are here," I whispered.

She looked at me. "I know."

She held her hand out to me. I squeezed it with all the fear I had. I felt Rob's body relax. I leaned over and whispered in his ear. "You have to stay awake for me please."

He looked up at me with tired eyes. He did not look like a sixteen year old. He looked about five years older.

There's nothing we could do to stay safe. As me and Shellie found out in the past, running will make him chase us. We just aren't fast enough. His footsteps came closer and stopped next to us. Shellie's eyes filled with tears, Rob didn't stay awake, and I could feel a brave side in me starting to come out. Everything became quiet. One of the top crates fell and hit Shellie's head. She fell motionless to the floor next to me. Now that I felt alone, my bravery started to subside. My fear came back and I could feel that he knew I was scared.

The crates started moving quietly at first, and then they started falling to the outside, creating an opening. I could see dad, and I tried to move to the opposite side of where he was. He reached his arm in and a crate fell on top of it. That's when I started climbing the opposite side and was able to run to my doggie. I heard his footsteps behind me. He grabbed my arm and threw me to the ground. He came on top of me.

"Shellie," I screamed. "No," I said fighting him off. "Don't do this."

"Mattie," Shellie said in a daze.

"Shellie."

He threw my doggie to the side and roughly kissed my neck. Tears were now rolling down my cheeks. They were tears of pain, hatred, fear and vulnerability. I never found the strength to fight him off. There was blood on his arm from where the crate fell. I could feel it drip onto me, but didn't care.

"Shellie," I said tired. I didn't think she could hear me. I could hear him undo his buckle and take mine off. My strength somehow came back. I started to struggle, but he held my shoulders down. It hurt so much. I was looking to the sidewall and could finally hear crates move. "Shellie, please, help me."

"Mattie," I heard over crates moving. I looked to the pile of crates and reached for my doggie. I saw Shellie and reached for her.

"Shellie," I said weak and scared. She ran over and was trying to get his hands off my shoulders. "Just call the police, then you can help me."

He started going faster. I heard more crates move and Rob was standing up. I looked to him. "Rob."

"Mattie," he ran over. "Get off her."

He was able to lift dad's hand off my shoulder and I used dad's shoulders to get out from under him.

Shellie was no longer on the phone. Rob was now dealing with dad. Shellie was holding me and I was holding her arm. She pulled a blanket over me and ran her fingers through my hair. I heard many footsteps and saw the police grab dad. Rob had somehow ended up on the bottom. A policewoman knelt down next to me. "Hi girls. My name is Carol. What's yours?"

"Mattie," I said in shock and looking at Rob, still holding onto Shellie's arm. He wasn't moving again. "Rob."

"Mattie, this lady wants to help us and Rob. Come one, let's sit you up."

"I don't have a shirt on," I said still frozen and still looking at Rob.

"You can keep the blanket on," Carol said.

"Mattie, come on. This lady will help you. Mommy always helped us. This lady wants to help you like mommy did."

I tore my eyes away from Rob and looked at Carol. She looked very much like mom did. I sat up quickly and wrapped my arms around her neck. "I want you to help me."

I felt Carol wrap her arms around me, and Shellie's hand on my shoulder. I buried my face in Carol's shirt and let the tears roll.

"Can I stand you up?" Carol asked, then gently pushed me away and wrapped the blanket around my shoulders. Her and Shellie helped me up. The three of us walked to the police car. I stopped half way and turned around. There were still policemen surrounding Rob. His legs hadn't moved.

"You can go see him. Let's have you cleaned up first okay?"

Carol led us to an ambulance and Shellie helped me up and inside. There was a woman inside with blue gloves on. I sat on the bed and the lady closed the door.

"Hi Mattie. Your sister told me your name. My name is Sherri. All I am going to do is clean you up. I am very sorry this happened to you. Can you tell me about your sister?" she asked with a smile.

"I want to know if Rob is okay. He saved me."

"You can see him as soon as I am done here."

I looked to Shellie and held my hand out. She came over and lightly held it. I felt the tingly bad feeling come back and started tearing up again. My breathing was starting to pick up. Shellie came over and touched my hair, and reminded me it was the lady in the ambulance.

Soon the lady gave me clothes. They were a little big, but they were very comfortable. I went over to the group of policemen. Shellie held my hand as we went over. I saw his legs moving and went to his head. I touched his hand.

"Rob, thank you."

He smiled and looked to me. I gently lifted his head and shoulders. "The three of us are going to the hospital." He was out of it, between the withdrawal, and what just happened, and everything else. I hugged him close. "Everything will be alright now."

Paramedics came and took over. Shellie and I rode in the ambulance with Sherri and Rob.

The three of us were taken to the same room. They put room in the bed, and Shellie and me had chairs. "We did it Shellie. He's gone. He will never find me again. He will never hurt us again." She brought me into a hug. I could feel her start to shake. I held her tighter then let her go. She was going into a panic attack. The room did have two beds. Shellie was able to get herself on the mattress. "Shh, shh, just relax. Go to sleep. I will be here when you wake up. It's okay."

When she went to sleep I went over to Rob. I touched his cheek and he slowly turned his head to face me. "Open your eyes."

He slowly opened them and looked at me. I lay down next to him. "Thank you."

"Stop Mattie."

"What?"

"It's my job, to protect you. It's always been my job."

I had gone to sleep, and when I woke up I saw Carol in the chair. She looked up at me. "Hi Mattie."

"Hi Carol," I said tired.

"You okay?"

"Yes, just scared. I had another bad dream."

"I know you did. Listen, how would you feel if I took you guys in?"

"Like adopting us?"

"Well, it would be a foster home. Just a home where you three can come, feel safe and feel loved," she explained.

"I would appreciate that. I'm sure Shellie and Rob would too. They should be awake soon."

"Oh, I'm in no rush. I can wait."

I sat in the chair next to Carol and we talked. She asked me questions about my life, and some were too painful to talk about.

I looked at Shellie, knowing she was the one that kept me alive. Her leg moved and I went over to her and touched her cheek.

"Mattie?"

"It's me. Officer Carol is here," I told her. "She is going to foster us until we can get back on track."

"Would you really do that for us?"

"Of course I would," Carol said. Shellie got up and went over to Carol. She stood up and Shellie gave her a huge hug.

"Thank you so much," Shellie said.

We were released from the hospital two days later, and Carol was taking us to her house. The house was beautiful, but she had a husband that I tried to stay away from. I mean he was nicer then dad ever was, but I just can't trust him. I can't trust them ever again.

I was still having nightmares. Rob was now clean from drugs and alcohol, as was I. Carol was spoiling us in ways I didn't understand.

I guess Rob or Shellie had told Carol about my birthday because it was one of the best birthdays ever. I really missed mom on my birthdays, but Carol was able to fill in the gap a little.

CHAPTER 18

I hadn't realized I had gone to sleep until woke up. I sat up from Rob's lap and looked around. I had forgotten where I was. Rob put his hand on my cheek. "Hey sweetie."

"Hey Rob, what time is it?"

"Does it really matter anymore?"

"I guess it doesn't," I smiled. "Where is Shellie?"

"In here," she yelled from across the house.

It had been two months to the day since my horrible incident. I could feel my body changing, and not in good ways. I woke up one morning and felt so nauseous. I ran to the bathroom and threw up. I heard Shellie come into the bathroom. "Is Carol awake?"

"Carol," she yelled.

"Shellie, please go check."

I heard footsteps coming up the stairs. "Mattie, you okay?"

"No, I just got sick," I said turning my head to Carol.

"You've been eating okay. Let's see how you feel the rest of the day."

Through out the day I was feeling cramps, but haven't gotten my period for two months. I told Shellie and we came to the conclusion that I was pregnant. The only person that ever went down there was my father.

"Shellie, I…I can't have this baby. It's his. I am not going through with it."

Carol had gotten us pregnancy tests and every time I tested, it was positive.

Rob came in and saw the test strips. "Mattie, I'm sorry."

"What are you sorry?" I asked through fallen tears.

"I didn't help you in time. I let him hurt you," he said.

"No," I said walking to him. "None of this is anyone's fault, except his. I'll just get an abortion."

Carol came over to me. "I know this is hard for everyone here, but you know that this baby might change everything. Why don't we just go through with it? I know the remainder of the pregnancy will be tough, but it will change your life," she smiled.

Shellie came over and wrapped her arms around me. I let the tears fall while I was laying the comforting embrace of my sister.

7 months pass
October 12, 2007

I was going into labor as we were getting things packed into the car. Rob picked me up and sat in the back with me. Shellie sat at my feet, holding my hand.

Once we got to the hospital it took no more than ten minutes to get me into a room. The doctor who was keeping an eye on me through out the nine months came into the room. I was only half way to being able to get the baby out. The contractions were getting closer and within a few hours I was ready.

It was in no ways easy, but the baby is out, and I am feeling weaker than ever.

"She's bleeding out," the doctor said. I could feel frantic in the room. My sister's expression changed.

"What do you mean she's bleeding out?"

"She's loosing more blood than what her body is producing. This happens for various reasons. We are trying our best to make it stop."

I was looking at my sister, as a tear trickled down my cheek. I saw tears forming in her eyes. "Don't be scared Shellie. I knew this was going to happen."

"You knew?"

"I knew my body wasn't going to be able to handle this. I've been through so much, and with what happened nine months ago, my body will never recover."

"What are you saying?" she asked.

"Sissy, it's time."

"No it's not," she pleaded.

"I know we just found each other, we found a home and things were looking brighter, but not for me."

"You're a fighter, you always have been."

"I've done my fighting Shellie. It's time. You know this is better for me."

Carol came up behind Shellie and put her hands on Sissy's shoulders. I could see tears in her eyes.

"I can't," Shellie said.

"Shellie, my life has been too hard. My body has never really recovered from any of it." I looked at my doctor. "Please, just let me go."

He stopped and didn't take the next tool from his assistant. He slowly stood up and came over to me. He kissed my forehead and quietly shuffled the other doctors out of the room. The door lightly closed and the grip on my hand tightened. Shellie sat on the bed next to me.

"Shellie, I am going to see mom again. It's not all bad. I'll be safe. You have to know that you are safe too. You have Carol and Rob. I looked at Rob. "I wish we could have grown old together."

He put his hand to my head. "You rest now."

7:47 pm

I looked up at the ceiling as tears were running into my hairline. Shellie put her hand on my heart. I weakly looked at her as she started fading in and out of my vision. I felt my eyes closing, but couldn't fight it off. I then realized this wasn't sleep.

I woke up to a bright light and heard my sister. I turned to my side and was looking down on her. I was in heaven. I looked back down to my sister hugging my lifeless body, and Carol holding my newborn daughter.

"What are we going to name her?"

"Mattie," my sister said.

I slowly stood up and looked around at my home for eternity. I slowly moved my feet and came to a beautiful tree. I saw a human figure standing next to the tree. As I got closer the person turned around. She smiled a beautiful smile, just as I remembered it.

"Mom."

Would you like to see your manuscript become a book?

If you are interested in becoming a PublishAmerica author, please submit your manuscript for possible publication to us at:

acquisitions@publishamerica.com

You may also mail in your manuscript to:

**PublishAmerica
PO Box 151
Frederick, MD 21705**

We also offer free graphics for Children's Picture Books!

---

www.publishamerica.com

CPSIA information can be obtained at www.ICGtesting.com
Printed in the USA
BVOW001503170513

321026BV00001B/58/P